Sea, Sky, Islands

Sea, Sky, Islands

Three Stories

Alice K. Boatwright

The author gratefully acknowledges the journals in which these
stories originally appeared:
Enterzone ("Between the East and Tomorrow" under the title of
"Reading Raymond Carver")
Amarillo Bay ("Life Sentences")
Beloit Fiction Journal and *America West* ("Divas")

Noontime Books
San Francisco, CA
info@noontimebooks.com

ISBN: 978-0-9916185-7-6

Book design: Sue Trowbridge

For Jim, with love

Contents

Between the East and Tomorrow

When Janet Emory and Tom Morrison drove through Port Angeles, Janet looked at every house, wondering which one Raymond Carver had lived in. They had been driving for two days, up from San Francisco, and Port Angeles, lying between the snow-capped Olympics and the blue sea, was the most prosperous town they had seen in hours. Houses climbed the hillside and clustered around the harbor where bright-colored fishing boats were moored, and big cranes slanted against the sky.

"I bet it's up there," said Janet, pointing to some houses sheltered by tall blue-black firs.

"No, it's out that way," said Tom, nodding toward the far end of town.

Tom was an attorney and could make everything he said sound like a fact. Even when Janet knew he didn't really know what he was talking about, she found it hard not to believe him.

"What makes you say that?" she asked.

"It has the best view," he said.

"I don't think Carver was the 'best view' type."

"Why not – if he could afford it?"

Janet shrugged. Tom had never even read Raymond Carver. She had just graded forty-six freshman compositions on "Cathedral" and almost felt like she had been living with Carver, not Tom, for the past week. After so much time poring over his words, it was amazing to think that the man himself might have walked down this street.

When they planned this trip Janet had imagined what it would have been like to meet him – she had different scenarios – but of course that was impossible. At her last class she'd read the poem "Gravy" about how grateful he was for his life even though he was dying young. She was the only one who cried, but of course, to her students, 50 years old was not young.

Tom pulled into a gas station, and, while he filled the tank, Janet walked up and down trying to memorize every detail of the place. She didn't believe in taking photographs: they just made you lazy about really looking. Being there.

She would have liked to go down to the harbor, maybe sit in a coffee shop and read the local newspaper, but Tom said they didn't have time. Within minutes they were back in the car, and Port Angeles had disappeared.

Janet sat with her back against the door, looking at the road behind them.

"What's the matter?" Tom asked.

"Oh, I don't know," she said, picking at a loose yarn on her sweater. Even though she had known she wouldn't see Raymond Carver, she had expected something. But what.

* * *

Janet and Tom were on their way to spend a week in the San Juan Islands, not doing anything special, just resting and enjoying the view. Lately they had not been getting along very well, so being together, in a cabin on an island, would be a strenuous activity.

It took several more hours and two ferries to get to their destination, but they finally arrived, driving the last mile down a road so overgrown it was like a green tunnel. When they came out, there was their house on a small spread of lawn that ran right down to the beach.

The house was perfect, just as Janet had imagined it, small and neat, with every window framing woods, sea, sky, islands. She rushed out onto the deck and leaned against the rail. "Smell the air," she said, when Tom came out to join her. The cool breeze was moist and scented by fir and salt, not the city smells: pavement and exhaust.

For a moment they stood together, then Tom went back inside. He started up the coffeemaker, while Janet began unpacking. After the long trip, it felt good to restore a sense of domestic order. The smell of coffee filled the house as she lay their sweaters in the closet and hung their rain jackets on hooks by the door.

"I'm ready for some rain!" she said, slipping her feet into rubber clogs and doing a little dance.

Janet and Tom had moved to California from Boston only a few months before, and Janet was already tired of sunshine. She found the brightness oppressive and the fog – which she associated with rain – disappointing.

The northwest, she had announced to Tom as they crossed the Columbia River, was more to her taste. The simplicity of the landscape was soothing: round humped islands, tall straight trees, billowing clouds, water. There were no pink, green, or lavender homes, no neon signs, no palms, no garish flowers. Even the grass was less gaudy.

This is more like it, she had said, although she wasn't sure what it referred to.

* * *

"We need to go shopping," said Tom, his head in the refrigerator. He was throwing away things left by previous tenants that he didn't approve of: relish, yellow mustard, margarine.

Janet hated to see food thrown away, but she only said: "Start a list." She was stripping her clothes off to lie in the sun. It had been a long time since she had been anywhere she could sunbathe nude and she felt self-conscious, stepping out into the light naked. The cool air touched her breasts and belly. She lifted her arms and let the breeze blow all around her, then lay down carefully on the cold plastic stripping of a lounge chair.

"What are you doing?" asked Tom.

"Having a clean air bath. Why don't you join me? It's great."

"No thanks." He sat down with his coffee and spread out the newspaper. "If you don't put on sunscreen, you'll get cancer," he said.

"OK," said Janet, stretching. The sun felt warm and soothing, not lethal, and the breeze stroked her skin.

Tom frowned at her and lifted the newspaper between them.

Janet closed her eyes, remembering the night two years ago when she had run into Tom with some friends from high school at a pub on Charles Street. They hadn't run across each other for years, and she'd been surprised by how glad he was to see her. He'd been a good-looking popular senior when she was a freshman and she'd hardly known him, but when he slipped his arm around her, it had felt just right – like they'd always belonged together.

Janet still believed in that moment of recognition, but since they'd arrived in California, it seemed harder and harder to find things to say. They had made love exactly twice, and then it had been very matter-of-fact, nothing like the way it used to be. The way she remembered it when she was alone. Maybe, thought Janet, who had recently turned 30, this was part of getting older. Still, she looked down at her pale legs and turned them from side to side trying to arrange them in a way that looked appealing.

Tom set down the newspaper, but he didn't look at her. He gazed at something in the water. After a moment he went inside and came back with binoculars. He lifted them to his eyes and stood silent and motionless for what seemed like forever.

"What is it? What are you looking at?" asked Janet.

"Otters," he said.

"No kidding!"

Janet got up and Tom handed her the glasses, but as she scanned the blurry water, he put his hand on her back and his touch was so cool and impersonal, she pulled away.

"I didn't see them," she said, putting down the glasses.

"That's because you didn't look where I showed you," he said. He sat down again, leaving her feeling naked and foolish.

Janet went inside to dress. When Tom came in she was still standing at the bureau, a t-shirt in each hand, trying to decide, brown or blue.

"Let's go shopping," he said. "I'm hungry."

* * *

The road to town wound by rolling meadows where sheep grazed, past silvered beaches, and through dark stretches of forest. Each time they rounded a bend and came to a new scene of islands and water, mountains and sky, Janet said: "Isn't this amazing?" and, for a change, Tom didn't say I told you so, but smiled and said yes.

In town they shopped at the one grocery store and

explored the narrow streets where useful shops vied for space with gift galleries and cafes serving espresso.

"I'd like to live here forever," said Janet, looking at a display of handspun yarn in a shop window.

"That's what you said about San Francisco before we moved there," said Tom.

"Did I?" asked Janet. "Did I really?"

But Tom had already disappeared into the bookstore.

The bookstore was in an old house right on the water, and Janet wandered the aisles, imagining that she was the owner, leading a simple life in the cool damp quiet. All through college, she had worked as a bookstore clerk. Then it had seemed like a pleasant way to acquire books cheaply and pay the rent until she was ready to start teaching. Now after several years of trying to herd indifferent and rebellious students toward literature, waiting on customers who wanted to read sounded wonderful.

A new edition of Raymond Carver's collected stories was displayed prominently on a table by the door. Janet picked it up, enjoying the soft colors and silky feel of the dust jacket, the rough cut edges of the paper, the clean spare design of the pages – so like the stories themselves. On the back was the familiar brooding face she was sure she would have recognized anywhere.

She examined the table of contents and was still debating over whether to splurge and buy the hardcover, when Tom came up, took a copy, and carried it to the counter.

"What are you doing?" asked Janet.

"Buying a book," he said.

"But why are you buying that book?"

"Obviously so I can read it."

Janet watched him make his purchase, amazed at the surge of resentment she felt. She had no doubt that by nightfall she would hear Tom's expert opinion on Carver's work, as well as his living habits.

"Come on, Janet, let's go home and eat," he said, opening the door.

Janet turned away from him, her heart pounding angrily, and went to the back of the store. There she stood between the shelves of books, pretending to look for something while her eyes filled with tears. It was stupid, she knew, but she couldn't help it.

After a few minutes she was able to compose herself. Then she bought her own copy of the book and carried it out to the car where Tom sat drumming his fingers against the steering wheel.

On the way home, the two books in their thin paper bags lay on the seat between them. Janet was acutely aware of their separateness as she looked out blindly at the passing scene.

"So why did you buy that book?" asked Tom. "Now we have two copies."

"I was already planning to buy it. You should have waited and read mine," said Janet, trying not to sound sulky.

"But you weren't buying it. You were just looking at it," he argued. "How long do you think I should wait for you to make up your mind?"

Janet didn't know what to say. The question, she was sure, was not really about the book. And anyway, Tom was an attorney. He never asked a question he didn't already have the answer to.

* * *

Once the groceries were stowed away and they had eaten, the afternoon stretched before them like the empty sea. Janet hunted through a shelf of battered paperbacks and took several out to her chair on the deck. Tom sat down beside her with the Carver book and began reading, methodically starting with the first story.

Janet still felt bruised, but she told herself that silence was preferable to shouting. Lately they had seemed to slip into endless rounds of shouting that made her wonder what she had done to her life.

Her friends and family had all been shocked when she told them that Tom had accepted a position with a firm in San Francisco and that she was going to move with him.

"But your whole lives are here," her older sister exclaimed.

"We'll make a new one," Janet had said, feeling like a pioneer, and she had actually enjoyed the process of moving. But once they were in their new apartment, she found herself in a state like permanent jet lag. At night she couldn't sleep and during the day she spent half her energy fighting the desire to lie down. Everything seemed unfamiliar – not just the weather, the flowers, and the architecture – but the labels on food, the meaning

11

of words, the expressions on people's faces. She tried to explain to Tom how lost she felt, but he was busy with his job and wouldn't admit to sharing any of the same feelings.

"Nothing's changed," he insisted. All she needed to do was make up her mind to be happy and they'd be fine. Janet had tried, but loneliness was like a stitch in her side that never went away.

* * *

"Would you like me to read to you?" Tom asked. Janet was two murders into an Agatha Christie, but he sounded conciliatory, even friendly, so she nodded and closed her book.

He began slowly but, as the story of a wife who struggles to reach her husband unfolded, his cheeks flushed and he picked up speed. There were no sounds except his voice and the soft slap of waves hitting the beach.

Janet, who recognized the story and knew it ended with the wife praying to God for help, grew tense anticipating the intimate words coming from his lips; and she was reminded of the day a few weeks ago when she had come home from teaching to find Tom waiting for her, his face pale and his angry eyes like stones.

"I've been reading this!" he said, shaking the notebook she used as a journal in her face.

"Sometimes I think I should never have come here," he read, mimicking her. "I'm so unhappy I don't know what to do. I wonder if I only moved with Tom because I was afraid to be alone. . ."

Janet had been too shocked either to defend herself or to accuse him of violating her privacy. She had simply grabbed the notebook, thrown it into the kitchen sink, and dropped matches on it until it burst into flames.

"Do you think that fixes anything?" said Tom, watching her. "Do you really think now we'll both stop knowing how you feel?"

By the time Tom got to the story's last line, Janet felt like she was choking. She stood up quickly, the aluminum frame of her chair squawking loudly, paperbacks falling to the deck.

"What's the matter?" Tom asked.

"That story's just so sad," she said, moving to the railing. "Sometimes the sadness takes me by surprise."

Tom pushed his own chair away from the table carefully.

"I liked it," he said. "I thought it was pretty good." Then he yawned and ran his fingers through his hair until it stood out around his head in curly clumps.

"I'm going to lie down now," he said and went inside. This was not, she knew, an invitation to join him.

* * *

Janet watched him through the window as he sat down on the bed, bent to take off his shoes, and then lay down flat on his back. Each motion was economical, discrete, like a frame in a motion picture. She could see herself too, reflected in the window, looking tense and solitary against a backdrop of islands, ocean, and big Western sky.

Now that she was alone, Janet thought she ought to be able to relax, but the silence was so deep, she felt like she'd gone deaf. Even the water seemed to have stopped moving. Long shadows had begun to creep across the lawn and the layers of islands were darkening from green to black. She shivered at the thought of the long evening ahead, and the stitch of loneliness tightened under her ribs as if someone were pulling on a thread getting ready to knot it off.

Tonight, she told herself as she gathered up the damp paperbacks, it would be cold enough for a fire in the fireplace, and that would give them something to do, something to talk about. And there was still dinner to cook and eat and clean up. So the day would pass and then there would be six more and then the drive back. And then what. What would she do.

She stood in the doorway, looking at Tom and wondered if he too were secretly somewhere else: suspended between the life they had once had and the future.

As she lay down beside him, the bed sagged and creaked. She settled herself, careful to preserve the space between them. Then she reached for her new book and folded it in her arms against her chest. The weight of it was comforting, and, as she held it, she felt all the sad stories, the clamoring voices, prayers, and dreams flow into her, along with Carver himself writing – and living

14

– his way out of his own sad story until he could say he had been a lucky man.

She closed her eyes and saw the tall cranes, the snow-capped mountains. She was leaning idly against the car, watching the morning shoppers go by, when she caught sight of him. He was coming down the street, his clothes rumpled from hours of writing, his expression calm and distracted, and any minute now, any minute, she would join him.

Life Sentences

Jack Hillyer waited on the deck while the Masons made a last tour of the house. He studied the scene below him: Easton, tucked against its curving harbor with a ferry standing at the dock, the pale green landing strip carved between dark woods and golden meadows, and, beyond, other islands floating like green hummocks on the shining water.

The cove where he and Patti lived was down to the left, hidden from this vantage point, but he knew exactly where it was and could picture everything in its place: The woods, the cabin, the patch of garden, and Patti. He set Patti on the porch, reading in the butterfly chair, her legs folded up, long red hair pulled back with a rubber band. Not that she was a big reader, but he had seen her that way one afternoon and liked the image. He carried it in his memory like the faded photograph of his two children that he kept in his wallet. He would call it up and say to himself, 'This is Patti, the woman I love.'

He glanced at his watch and took out his cell phone to let her know he'd be home soon, but the muffled sound of a door closing made him put away the phone and turn back to the house instead.

Through the large kitchen windows, he could see Gina Mason opening cupboard doors and examining appliances. Bill Mason was talking, his hands turned palm up beating the air emphatically. Finally she stopped and leaned against the dishwasher, her arms crossed. Something about the set of her cheeks told Jack that they would not make an offer on this house.

He did not want to appear impatient, so he sat down on a wooden deck chair and took a few deep breaths. Although it was still August, the air had changed. Autumn was coming and then winter would follow – the long slow season when no one even came to the island, much less bought a house here.

The Masons had looked at six houses that day, and they seemed no closer to making a choice than they had first thing in the morning. They were management consultants from Seattle and wanted a place to get away from the city. "We want a simple life," Gina said, gesturing as if to wave away their shiny new Range Rover with its bicycle and ski racks. Bill, who compulsively checked his iPhone, wanted a view of the water; she wanted privacy and a garden – all of which Jack had offered them in different packages but so far nothing had clicked.

This house was on a high bluff and had been beautifully crafted from cedar and glass. Inside, Bill had smiled as he touched the raised paneled doors and hand-planed window frames. He paced off rooms and pointed out to his wife that she could have a desk in front of a window looking out at Puget Sound. He asked a lot of questions about the thickness of the insulation and the location of boundary lines, but Gina just ran the pointed toe of her leather boot over the carpet, watching the pile shift.

"I don't want wall to wall," was all she said.

Earlier they had looked at an old farmhouse set at the edge of a meadow full of late summer flowers. There she had stood on the porch a long time, watching the wind in the grass, while her husband waited by the car, jingling his keys in his pocket and asking Jack about sewage treatment on the island.

Jack had met a lot of people like the Masons. They came to the island for a vacation and thought it was heaven. Right away they wanted to buy a piece of it. Of course, they had no idea what it was really like to live here. The ferry trips to the mainland. The rainy winters. The unreliable electricity. The wind and silence. And then suddenly, with spring, backpackers and bicyclists everywhere underfoot.

Jack understood and accepted these things; his family had been sheep farmers and fishermen here for more than a hundred years, and he liked to imagine – somehow – that they'd stay a hundred more. He had only left the island once for more than a few days, and that had been

21

back when he was drinking and thought he should see the world. Unfortunately he could only guess where he'd been from the matchbooks he found in his pockets when he finally made his way home.

Bill Mason came back out on the deck, with Gina trailing behind him. She was in her late thirties, her round body disguised in expensively layered clothes. He was a good-looking man, about Jack's age – forty-five – and the type who looked just right in a tweed jacket.

"What did you say the tax rate was again, Hillyer?" he asked.

Jack told him and his fingers flew over his calculator. He nodded as he saw the results.

Jack felt a flicker of hope.

"Many people commute?"

Jack nodded. "You can see the airport from here," he said, pointing to the green landing strip below, "and the ferry system is excellent. It's still an island, of course."

"Yes," said Mason, surveying the cedar facade of the house with its sharply slanted roof and expanses of glass. "My wife and I like that."

He said the words "my wife" with an unconscious confidence of possession that Jack was sure he'd never feel again about any woman.

"Is there anything else you want to see today?" he asked, keeping his voice neutral. He tried not to judge his clients, but he could size up pretty quickly which ones were hoping for a change that a new house would not provide. His ex-wife Shirley still believed that they'd be together today if only they'd gotten off his damn island.

She meant to make him mad calling it that. Which just goes to show.

Still he had tried, in his way, to make the marriage work. He'd given up farming and gone into real estate like she wanted him to, but in some ways the jobs weren't that different: he could still work his ass off seven days a week and not make a dime.

Mason put his iPhone into the inside pocket of his jacket. He glanced at Gina, who shook her head just slightly. "No thanks," he said. "I guess that's it for today."

Tomorrow perhaps they could see the other end of the island, Mason suggested. They'd like to see a few more places. Something with more gardening potential, he added, pointing out the steep slope of the bluff.

"Private though," said Gina.

"Of course. No problem," Jack said. "We've got plenty of places like that around here." He'd noticed people who came from the mainland always talked a lot about privacy. For some, the solitude the island offered was more dazzling than the views.

The cabin he lived in was at the end of a long wooded road with no other houses nearby, and when Patti first moved in, she couldn't sleep for the quiet. She'd grown up in a high-rise in Manhattan where the noise never stopped. Now in the morning, she would walk outside naked and stand in the yard like a deer – completely at one with the landscape and unaware of its beauty.

Bill Mason was taking pictures of the view, his camera clicking repeatedly to capture all 180 degrees of ocean, islands, and sky. If he'd been alone, Jack thought he might have bought this house.

He stuck out his hand to Gina Mason. "Until tomorrow then?"

"Until tomorrow," she said. Her hand lay in his like a filleted fish, but he shook it firmly. If he could sell them a house, his winter would be in the bag. Bill Mason was jingling his keys again, ready to leave.

"You go on ahead," Jack told them. "I have to lock up."

They looked relieved and got into their car quickly. Jack waved and they waved back, but he saw them begin to argue before they were even out of sight. No doubt he would receive a message later saying "urgent business" had called them back to Seattle. He didn't envy them.

* * *

As soon as they were gone, he called home, but the line was busy. That was surprising because Patti always said she had no friends on the island except him. They had met at an AA meeting earlier in the summer. She had appeared at the Fellowship Hall one night in June, introduced herself as "Patti, addict, alcoholic," and she'd been around ever since.

Jack had been fascinated by her quiet manner, her long red braids, and delicate tattoos. He asked her out for coffee to welcome her to the group. She said OK and after that one thing had led to another.

His friends in the program said it was wrong to get involved with a newcomer, especially a young woman, but Jack didn't think of Patti as young most of the time. She said she'd stopped counting birthdays ever since she turned 20, and the things she knew shocked him – made him feel like he was the one with no experience. She said she'd come to the island because she got on the wrong bus in Seattle. She'd meant to go to San Francisco, but when she saw the water, the mountains, and the islands she hopped a ferry and that was all there was to it.

Shirley was disdainful about the whole relationship. If Jack bumped into her at the grocery or the post office, she would curl her lips back and say "Jack," in a tone that wrapped greeting, recrimination, and goodbye into one. She called Patti "that whore who's got you wrapped around her little finger."

He didn't care what she thought. She had gotten the house and everything in it, while he was living in a rented cabin. He was paying her alimony and the kids' school tuition, so the way he figured it, he didn't owe an explanation to anyone.

Not that she could ever in a million years understand what he and Patti had going anyway. At the sight of her puffy face, red with indignation, Jack believed that he had never loved her in twenty-one years as much as he had loved Patti in these past months. They had known each other since kindergarten and nothing about her could surprise him, while everything Patti said and did was filled with mystery.

Patti didn't confide in him that much when they were alone, but at meetings, sitting around stained card tables in the Fellowship Hall's dim light, she would say things that made the back of his neck prickle with love and compassion for her. It was one of the things that made him look forward to meetings now. Wondering what Patti might say next. Before that, staying sober had been something he knew he had to do if he didn't want to die at fifty like his father. He had trouble remembering why he was doing it when he sat alone every evening in the cabin.

Now he and Patti were regulars at the Wednesday and Saturday meetings, arriving early to set out the chairs and staying late to wash the coffee cups. "Our dates," Jack called these nights out, because Patti didn't like any of his friends from his married days, and there was nowhere to go on the island, not even a movie theater.

Sometimes he'd take her around to different houses and ask her which one she'd like them to buy, as he ran his hands up inside her blouse and felt her cool smooth flesh.

That was just a game they played, but the reality was if he could sell one more house this season, he'd be able to take her to Hawaii on vacation that winter. He'd never done anything like that before, but with Patti, he wanted to. It was like the less she asked for, the more he wanted to give.

The night before they had sat up in bed looking at brochures filled with pictures of palm trees and white beaches, turquoise water and big pink hotels. The ocean was warm there, he told her, and she said it didn't matter because she couldn't swim.

"I'll teach you," he said. "It's natural, like breathing.

You'll love it," he promised, and she said, "OK, I'll love it," and turned out the light.

Jack was a little bit hurt by that, but he tried not to be. It was her style to be abrupt sometimes – a city style – and he had to get used to it. He knew there were things she had to get used to about him too. She thought it was weird that he had never wanted to go anywhere before.

His own children – born and raised here – didn't get that either, so why should she? They had left the island as soon as they were out of high school and hadn't spoken to him since.

"We don't want to be like you," Jessie said the last time he saw her. "We want to live in the real world."

Patti had laughed when he told her that story. "I thought they were in college," she said.

"They are," he said.

"That's not the real world," she said then she pushed him down into the pillows on their bed and covered his face with her long hair. Jack had closed his eyes as she kissed him all over, feeling exquisite gratitude that this bit of the real world had come to him.

He tried the phone again, but now there was no answer. She must be outside, he told himself, picturing her in the yard picking blackberries. The bushes around the yard were loaded with ripe fruit, and he had suggested that morning that they try to make a pie. Before she moved in with Jack, Patti said she'd been living on Triscuits and coffee. He wasn't much better: frozen this, take-out that, and cereal. Learning to cook had been a project they could share.

The kitchen in this house, with its pristine new appliances, just begged for someone to come and cook in it. As he walked from room to silent room, closing and locking the windows, Jack felt the longing and anticipation in those empty spaces. He touched the satiny woodwork. It was a great house, even though the drive was steep and would be a bitch in the winter.

Shirley had expected him to make a fortune in island real estate. "Places like this don't stay undiscovered forever," she'd said. "You've got to get in the game now to win."

Jack didn't like to think of the island as a game. His family was always after him to break up the acreage his father had left him and make them rich, but he wouldn't do it. Between his drinking and the divorce, he'd lost everything else, and he meant to hang on to that piece of land.

Patti thought the idea of owning land was funny. "It's just trees," she said, when he took her for a walk there. "How can you own a tree?" she asked, but later she told him that she could see from his face what it meant to him. He was at home there, at peace.

He had never loved her more than at that moment when he felt she saw him as he really was. This person who had lost nothing, because she'd never had anything.

Once he had washed her back for her. She had been sitting in the tub with a magazine and said, "Jack, would you wash my back for me?" Of course he said yes.

He knelt by the tub and rubbed her back with a washcloth. He could feel each bump of her spine, the flat triangles of her shoulder blades under her pale skin. Touching her like that made him think of Jessie, when she was a child. That kind of intimacy. It went beyond being together as a man and a woman.

Sometimes he was afraid to touch her. He'd put his hands out to her pull her narrow white hips toward his and feel afraid. She didn't seem to notice that any more than anything else. When she slipped into bed with him at night, maybe he could have been any guy, not Jack, the man who loved her. Who could tell with someone who had started drinking at nine, shooting drugs at thirteen?

Jack tried the cabin again and listened to the ringing phone with a sudden sharp pang of anxiety. He got into his car, turned the key, and the engine rattled into life. Dust flew and stones bumped against the under carriage of the car as he started down the drive. If he didn't sell this house before the autumn rains, it wouldn't move until spring. No one in his right mind would buy on this road when it was mud.

* * *

Driving fast kept his mind on the road, not the destination, and he made it across the island to the cabin in fifteen minutes flat. When he pulled into the yard, he could see right away that Patti was not outside. Not in the garden. Not picking berries. He bounded across the squeaky planks of the porch, past the empty butterfly chair, and pulled open the kitchen door.

"Patti?" he called, but there was no answer, and he

paused in the doorway listening to the silence. He didn't need to call again. The feeling an empty house gave off was one he knew all too well.

In the bathroom, he found their toothbrushes were still side-by-side in the glass on the sink. The new clothes he'd bought her were hanging in the closet. The book she had been reading lay on the bedside table, page 10 marked with a torn scrap of paper. Only the woven Nepali bag that she'd been carrying the night he met her was missing.

So why, in the pit of his stomach, did he believe she was not simply out, but gone?

He forced himself to sit at the kitchen table for 10 minutes his legs jiggling with tension then he went back through the cabin looking for clues to what she had done that day since he left for work. He felt foolish as he opened drawers and desperate as he peered under the bed, but he couldn't help himself.

If she were only going out, wouldn't she have let him know?

He thought back to breakfast, when he had last seen her. She had been sitting at the kitchen table, hunched over her bowl of cornflakes like a child, her tangled braids hanging over her shoulders, while he prattled on about his mother and aunts making blackberry pies every August. Wouldn't it would be fun.

Spoon in hand, she had glanced up at him with a blank look that reminded him of Jessie when she was a teenager. But then she had nodded. He was sure she had nodded.

He sat down again at the kitchen table across from her empty chair.

So was that it? Was that the warning? If he hadn't talked about blackberry pies would she still be here?

But even as self-pity rose up to defend him, he remembered other mistakes that added to the case against him. Times when he'd been short-tempered, pedantic, and dull. All those brochures about Hawaii. All those houses he made her visit. He'd imagined he was broadening her horizons, unselfishly helping her imagine a different kind of future unconnected to her past. But there was nothing unselfish about his love. He wanted her to picture a future with him in it.

He went to get a cold Coke out of the fridge and there, at last, he found his clue.

The ferry schedule was stuck to the door with magnets, and on it he saw a penciled doodle next to the phone number for Island Taxi.

He was sure it had not been there before, but would Patti have taken a taxi?

Maybe, if she were worried that he might see her hitchhiking.

He touched the doodle with his finger, as if he could read in those restless circles her farewell message to him.

* * *

There was still an hour until the last ferry left the island. It was just possible she'd gotten as far as Easton and changed

31

her mind. At this very moment, she might be loitering on the dock wondering whether to call him.

He grabbed his keys, and the screen door slammed as he left the house and jumped back into the car. With the cold Coke bottle creating a damp place between his legs, he drove as fast as he dared along the curving road that followed the coast. Rocky beaches and yellow cattail-studded marshes went by in a blur. He hugged the centerline, watching for bicyclists, but flew past them without slowing down.

When he reached Easton, the back of his shirt was drenched with sweat. He glanced quickly right and left, right and left, while he negotiated his way along the busy route to the ferry landing. When he finally reached the parking lot, he had trouble opening his fingers to let go of the steering wheel.

It was getting dark; the long summer days were not so long any more. A crowd of tired, sunburned backpackers and bicyclists waited by the entrance gate, while a long line of cars heavily laden with children, dogs, and baggage snaked across the lot. Jack scanned the crowd repeatedly, but he saw no redhead with a Nepali bag.

As a last resort, he headed over to the ticket window and, before he even reached it, he could tell from Burt Kemp's expression what he would hear.

"She bought a one-way for the five o'clock," he said with a satisfied smile, which told Jack that Shirl and half the island had known Patti was gone before he did. No doubt they were delighted by this juicy news. Not that he gave a shit what they thought. What they thought they knew.

The only thing that mattered to him was knowing when she had known.

Had she kissed him goodbye as if it were an ordinary day, all the time knowing it wasn't? Knowing there would be no blackberry pies. No swimming lessons. No more date nights.

He drove home slowly, simultaneously dreading the silence of the cabin and longing to be in the place where they had lived together. When he sat down again at the kitchen table, his chest filled with an ache that did not seem survivable, the more so because he knew he would.

And even though he was shocked, he had to admit he had always known this day would come. He had just hoped every day to put it off one day more.

Patti had once told him that she'd never had a relationship that lasted longer than three months. He would have liked to be the first.

He turned off the lights inside and went out to the porch. The butterfly chair creaked and protested mournfully as he sat down – a much heavier weight than she had been. It was a dark night, overcast with no stars or moon, not even any shadows.

* * *

He didn't know how long he'd been sitting there when his phone rang.

His heart leapt at the sound, but he could see right away that it wasn't her.

Still it took a moment for him to give up hope and realize the person calling was Bill Mason. Jack was so disappointed that he had trouble pulling himself together to focus on what Bill was saying.

His words were both slurred and emphatic as he said: "I've been thinking about that house. The one with the view. I want it, and I'm willing to make a cash offer. Can you write that up that tonight? I have to leave for Seattle in the morning."

Jack heard himself say yes – it was what he always said to clients – but he was thinking about pronouns. The long walk between I and we and back again.

With Mason he ran through the details, then said he would prepare the papers and meet him in two hours.

"Great. We can have a drink together. We'll toast the future."

"Sure thing," said Jack. "That sounds good."

"You know, Hillyer, sometimes you just have to go for what you want and damn the consequences."

"Right," said Jack, "I agree," and then he rang off.

Inside he went to his desk and opened his laptop. As he typed in the figures on the offer form, he pushed away thoughts of Hawaii. He told himself he would use the money for something else. Something for himself. Like maybe it was time he started building a home on his own land. Something with cedar and plenty of windows. He didn't have to stay in this crappy cabin. He could move on too, but, if Patti came back, she would know where to find him.

When he reached the bottom of the form, he realized he had pulled up the wrong one. This one, created when he first started in real estate, had a slogan across the bottom that said "Buy Your Plot in Heaven Now." Shirley's idea of a marketing strategy.

He didn't want to take the time to re-do his work, so he printed the form and used a marking pen to carefully cross out the slogan. Then he placed the papers in a new envelope, took a shower, and changed his clothes. Dressing alone in the bedroom he already felt like he'd begun a different life from the one he woke up in.

As he drove to the hotel where the Masons were staying, he reminded himself to expect nothing. Bill Mason might have wanted the house two hours ago, with a few drinks under his belt, but he could already have changed his mind. He and his wife had not seemed like a couple on their last day. Then again he had never imagined that he and Patti were on their last day either.

In a meeting Patti once said, "Drinking may be a death sentence, but sobriety is a life sentence." Everyone had laughed, thinking she was being witty, but Jack could tell from her expression that she wasn't making a joke.

He pictured her now on a Greyhound, watching the dark landscape rush by, the Nepali bag on the seat beside her. Thinking what. Going where. He was hurt that she hadn't taken any of the things he gave her when she left, as if she didn't want to be reminded of the life they'd shared.

Maybe that was wrong, though. Maybe she would remember, just as he would. Before they met, he'd been drowning in self-pity, if not in booze. She'd been the wave that carried him to shore.

In the small parking lot, Jack got out of the car and stretched, taking a deep breath of the salt-tinged air. The sky had cleared, becoming luminous behind the tall evergreens that encircled the old mansion hotel. He walked up the stone path to meet his client. Who knew what might happen next. The day wasn't over yet.

Divas

From the liquid darkness of the channel that runs between our island and the mainland, a voice floats up to my open kitchen window. It is Maria Callas singing *Norma*. Or more precisely it is John out in the boat with his boom box. He is supposed to be catching fish, but unless the fish are opera fans, I don't think he'll hook anything.

"Casta diva, casta diva," she sings, exhorting the moon to bring us peace. The melody is slow and rolling like the waves that lap the shore.

A candle flickers on the kitchen counter, the only light in the room. I am cutting vegetables, and the shadows of my hands look enormous as I raise and lower the knife. Zucchini, onions, yellow squash, pea pods, and red wedges of tomato cascade from the cutting board into a hot pan as she hits the first high note. Rice steams quietly on the burner like the chorus.

The music fills me with nostalgia: John played this for me the first time I visited him at his house on Queen Anne Hill five years ago. "No one sings *Norma* like Callas," he whispered in my ear as we sat on his back stoop looking down at the twinkling lights of the city. In that moment, when he first kissed me, with the music wrapping around us in the warm summer night, we were Callas. There was no one like us.

Tonight the mood is elegiac. John is depressed. Or is it angry? I can't always tell what he's feeling when he gets a certain shutdown expression and goes out – sometimes for hours – to roam the island or fish, as he's doing tonight.

It has been two years since we announced at our wedding breakfast that we were not just going to the islands for our honeymoon – that we planned to live here. John would write full-time, we said, and I would raise sheep, spin, and dye my own yarn. We had a small grubstake – the advance on his first book – but all we needed was a start. If we were willing to live simply enough, we reasoned, we would get along.

"Ha!" I say now, using both hands to crush a clove of garlic with the side of my knife.

You're crazy, said our friends, and maybe they were right. Things have not turned out the way we thought. We have worked hard and practiced simplicity almost to the vanishing point, but we are still out of money.

"I could get a job at the plant again," John offered this morning at breakfast.

Last winter when we could see that our savings were dwindling, John pulled the cover over his typewriter and went to work at the island's fish packing plant so that I could stay home and build up my inventory for the summer craft fairs. The long tedious days left his hands chapped and aching, his body reeking of fish, his spirits raw.

"We could also sell the sheep," I countered.

"Don't be silly," said John. "That's like a fisherman selling his boat."

"Some of them have had to do it."

"It's the last resort," he said. "We're not there yet."

"Well, it's my turn to do something," I said, picking up the thin weekly paper and turning to the want ads with determination. "And I can get a job just as easily as you can."

"It would only be temporary," said John, repeating a phrase we have used often to keep our spirits up.

I found three ads for administrative assistants on the mainland and decided to apply for them all. After mulching the tomatoes and taking care of the animals, I prepared my resume and got out my good white blouse and navy skirt. As I looked through my drawer for a pair of pantyhose, I practiced positive thinking. I am well organized, I said to myself. I have good computer skills. I am sure to be hired.

"Commuting won't be bad," I told John when he came down from his office for lunch. He looked mournfully at my city clothes laid out on the bed. "I'll knit on the ferry, and I can shop for groceries off island. We'll save a lot that way."

"It's only temporary," John repeated.

He didn't say what he used to say: "As soon as the new book sells, we'll be fine." Or, "Once you get picked up by the big stores, we won't have to worry." After two years of trips to the post office, countless phone calls, and polite rejections, doubt has settled over us like fog.

I sprinkle soy sauce vigorously over the vegetables and clamp the lid down on the pan. "We are good at what we do," I say, giving the pan a shake. "We can make it. We will."

From outside, the voice of Maria Callas rises over the quiet singing of the chorus like the moon coming up over the trees. I can see the black shape of John's boat, and it reminds me of the orca whales that live in these northern waters. I imagine them drawn up by the sound of the music, arching their backs as they swim by.

The first time we went out fishing off the island, we found ourselves surrounded by a pod of whales. First one, then another, and another, and another of the sleek black-and-white bodies broke the surface, so that my excited words "Look, a whale!" stopped in my throat, and I clutched the sides of the boat, in awe. John cut the motor and put one hand over mine as we watched in silence, holding our breath. The boat rocked from side to side. We could see their eyes, hear the cavernous sound of their breathing, smell their breath. The beauty and danger lit John's face.

"Wee-ooo!" he stood up shouting when the last one had passed. "Wee-ooo!" His voice bounced off the surrounding islands and floated down the narrow passages of water.

Later it was the story we told everyone back home to explain what living on the island was like. What we didn't realize then was that the real dangers – impatience and resentment – traveled deep too, breaking the surface when we least expected it.

The music rises to a climax, stops, then begins again. "Casta diva," she prays.

"Casta diva," I sing along, setting out the placemats and plates.

It doesn't matter if we don't have fish. Even without electricity, I will cook dinner. Even if I have to work in an office, I will still have my sheep. This has been a season of "even withouts" – when expectations have shrunk like melting ice. It doesn't matter. Everything is all right.

The music comes to a close. A holy silence follows.

I open the kitchen door and peer in the direction of the water. I can't see John, but I can hear the rattle of oarlocks, the splash of oars as he approaches.

"Wee-ooo!" I shout into the darkness. "Wee-ooo!"

Acknowledgements

Love and thanks to the wonderful people who have been my creative fellow travelers for so many years: Janet Basu, David Boatwright, Kathy Chetkovich, Martha Conway, Michelle Dionetti, Marianne Faithfull, Mark Fishman, Ann Hill, Margaret Jones, Jim Mullins, Seamus O'Connor, Carol Sanford, Victoria Schultz, and the late Katie Supinski. Nothing I have written would ever have been finished without their gentle guidance and enthusiastic support.

In addition, special thanks to my collaborator on this project, Marsha Karr. Here we are together again, so many years after all those creative dreaming lunches in Berkeley.

Alice K. Boatwright is a widely published short story writer and author of *Collateral Damage,* three novellas about the Vietnam War from the perspectives of those who fought, those who resisted, and the family and friends caught in the crossfire between them. She is also author of the award-winning Ellie Kent mysteries. alicekboatwright.com
Author photo: Maria Aragon

Marsha Karr was raised on the vast Canadian prairies and her love for open landscapes is evident in the evocative paintings illustrating *Sea, Sky, Islands.* She now lives and works in the Pacific Northwest and Baja California Sur, Mexico. Her work has been shown in solo and group exhibitions internationally.
marshakarr.com
Author photo: David Rabinovitch

Noontime Books is an independent book publisher that specializes in engaging and entertaining literary fiction.

Titles available:

Thieving Forest by Martha Conway
Sugarland by Martha Conway
Sea, Sky, Islands by Alice K. Boatwright